엘리트 시선 40

카라꽃 그대

장현경 시집

엘리트출판사

카라꽃 그대

카라꽃 그대

장 현 경 시집

엘리트출판사

아름다운 꽃들의 이야기 2

입추가 지나면 곧 우수(雨水)가 온다. 만물이 생동하는 계절, 봄을 그려본다. 글쓰기에서는 자신의 노력과 관심이 중요하다. 즉 많이 읽고 쓰고 생각해야 좋은 글을 쓸 수 있다. 좋은 글을 쓰기 위해서는 뛰어난 직관력과 논리적 사고 그리고 그 정확한 표현이 필요하다. 끊임없는 글 창작은 논리적인 사고의 틀을 갖추게 하고 생각한 내용을 구체적으로 표현할 수 있는 능력을 길러준다.

시는 영혼의 양식이요, 시대를 비추는 거울이다. 이런 관점에서 시인에게 필요한 것은 진실한 언행과 아름다운 삶이다. 즉 인간 삶을 바탕으로 심금을 울리는 작품을 쓰는 일이 아닌가 한다. 이런 의미에서 꽃들의 이야기는 인간 삶을 묘사하려는 듯 슬픔, 열정, 유혹, 환생, 불타는 사랑 등을 주제로 담고 있다.

꽃을 보니 마음이 밝아지고 기분마저 좋아진다. 시인으로 움츠린 몸에 기지개를 켜며 사계절 지지 않는 꽃들의 이야기를 소재로 여기 한 권의 영역 시집을 다듬는다. 꽃들의 이야기가 이 어려운 시대를 견뎌내는 수많은 독자에게 위로와 희망, 감동이 되기를 기대합니다.

늘 따뜻한 성원을 보내주신 가족과 이웃의 지지에 고마운 마음 전하며 청계문학 가족 여러분의 건승을 빕니다. 나의 시편들을 만나는 존경하는 독자님께 건강과 행복이 늘 함께하시기를 기원합니다.

2021년 1월 청계서재(淸溪書齋)에서
자정(紫井) 장현경(張鉉景) 삼가 씀

카라꽃 그대

나는 꽃이다
내 이름은 카라

하양 핑크 자주
노란빛의 옷을 좋아하고

나는 순수하고
열정적이며
순결을 지향하고
천년의 사랑은 물론
생명력도 강하다

이것도 부족하여
'아무리 찾아도
그녀만 한 여자는 없네요'로
회자하고 있다.

Kara Flower Thyself

I am a flower
My name is Kara

White pink purple
I like yellow clothes

I'm pure
Passionately
In the direction of purity
Of millennial love
Have a strong vitality

In short supply
'No matter how hard I look for her,
there's no other woman like her'
It's well-known to everybody.

제1부 창포꽃을 찾아

제2부 한라산의 눈꽃

제3부 며느리밥풀꽃

제4부 드라큘라시미아꽃

제5부 성에꽃

제1부

창포꽃을 찾아

물가에 창포꽃
배경화면이 되어
그윽한 향기로
고즈넉이 피어있네!

금강초롱꽃

금강산에서
초롱초롱한 모습으로 태어나

함경남도와 강원도
고산 지대에서
뿌리 내리고 꽃이 피네

초롱불을 들고
약초를 캐러

한반도의 등줄기를
아우르네!

Gilded Lantern Flower

At Mt. Geumgang
Born with a limpid appearance

Hamkyungnamdo and Gangwondo
In the alpine zone
It's rooted and flowering

With a lantern
To pick up herbs

The back of the Korean Peninsula
Encompass!

자주받침꽃

가느다란 나뭇가지에
타원형 녹색 이파리

여기저기
맹아(萌芽)로 돋아나

꽃잎이 받침 되고
받침이 꽃잎 되어
서로 한 몸으로

자주색 꽃을 피워 올리며
그윽한 향기 흩날리네!

Purple Pedunculus Flower

On a thin branch
Elliptical green leaves

Here and there
It is born with a bud

Petals are supported
The support is petal
In one body

With purple flowers
That smell is blowing off!

모과나무꽃

봄에 피는 연분홍빛 꽃
앙증맞게 아름다워

수피(樹皮)에 흰무늬가
더욱 돋보이네

노랗게 잘 익은 모과
못생기긴 해도
차나 술 재료로 쓰이고

바구니에 담아
실내에 놓아두면

은은한 향기 배어 나와
기분이 상쾌하고

한방에선
질병 치료제로 쓰이네!

Quince Flower

A light pink flower in spring
It's beautiful and beautiful

The white pattern in the bark
More impressive

Yellow ripe quince
Ugly as it may be
It's used as tea or alcohol

In a basket
If you leave it indoors

A subtle scent
In a refreshing mood

In herb medicine
It's used as a cure for disease!

창포꽃을 찾아

한낮에
햇빛을 모아
곱게 태운다
끝머리 노랑 창포꽃 유난히 곱다

짙은 보랏빛 밤이 오면
호숫가에 마구 뿌려진 창포꽃
소곤대며 깜박거린다

새벽녘
연못가 창포 꽃송이에
간신히 걸린 그믐달

그 옛날 단오 때
창포물에 머리 감는 여인들의 모습

물가에 창포꽃
배경화면이 되어
그윽한 향기로
고즈넉이 피어있네!

Find the Iris Flower

In the middle of the day
In the sun
Burn finely
Be exceptionally fine with the yellow iris

When the dark purple night comes
A iris flower scattered by the lake
Whisper and blink

At dawn
The pond is a flower bud
The barely caught moon

In the old Dano
The women who wash their heads in the iris

A iris flower by the pond
In the background
With a deep scent
It's blooming quietly!

분꽃

저녁 이내를 머금고
어스름에 피어 아침까지

여름내 그윽한 향기로
빛의 그림자
딛고 온 꽃

겨우 아침에서야
햇빛을 기다리며
그리움을 주는 꽃

아득히 저 먼 길로
다시 밀려나 버린
내 유년의 분꽃

마음속에
소박하게 피어있네!

Marvel of Peru

In the evening
From dusk to morning

With a breathtaking scent
Shadow of light
A flower over

It's only in the morning
Waiting for the sun
A nostalgic flower

Far away from there
Re-pushed
My childhood flower

In one's mind
It's just blooming!

치자꽃 향기

6월이 오면
뜰 앞 담장 따라
치자나무 꽃봉오리가 하얗게
고개를 내밀고 있다

한여름 무더위에
초록빛 이파리 사이로 핀
탐스러운 겹꽃 송이

세상을 보려는 듯
산들바람에 향기를 흩날리며
활짝 핀 치자꽃
은은한 달처럼 빛나는구나

여름이 가고
찬 바람이 불면
고희(古稀)의 언덕 위에
주황빛 열매가
주렁주렁.

Gardenia Flower Aroma

When June comes
Along the front fence of the courtyard
The gardenia flower bud whites
Be holding out one's head

In the midsummer heat
Blooming between green leaves
Attractive double flower

As if to see the world
With a breeze of scent
A broad flower
You shine like a moon

Summer is over
When the cold wind blows
On the hill of the seventy years of age
The orange fruit
A tree in full bearing.

참나리꽃

개울가 산기슭에
참나리가 싹을 틔우고
숨을 쉰다

돋아나는 움이
봄을 반기고
참나리에 핀 여름을 노래한다

주황빛 머리
검은 점투성이 얼굴
주아(珠芽) 품어
광야의 표범인 양

꽃송이마다
야무진 꿈을 싣고
눈이 부신 햇살 따라

그 모진 나날을
기도를 하듯
세상을 향해 잠시 발걸음 멈추며
지켜보고 있네!

Tiger Lily Flower

At the foot of the creek
With the cherubs sprouting
Breathe

A springing sensation
Welcome to spring
Sing summers in the blues

Orange hair
A black dotted face
The bud will sprout
A leopard in the wilderness

Per flower bud
With a wild dream
To a dazzling sun

I've been through all these years
As if in prayer
And then paused for a moment
I'm watching!

계관화

암탉이 아니고
수탉

화려하고
위엄이 있다

저 멀리
높은 곳에서
머리 숙이며
우는 수탉의 볏

계관화(鷄冠花)로
보일 듯 말 듯.

Cockscomb Flower

Not a hen
Rooster

Glamorous
Have dignity

Far away
At a high point
Bowing one's head
Rooster's crest

By cockscomb flower
Like you can see.

원추리꽃

세찬 비바람에
근심을 잊게 하는 여러해살이풀
물먹은 꽃잎으로 뙤약볕에도
싱그럽고 아름답다

칼날처럼 좁고 긴 이파리
두 줄로 마주나
서로 춤추고

외줄기 꽃대에서
깔때기 모양의 등황빛 꽃들이 싱글벙글
끝이 여러 개로 갈라지며
기다림에 지친 내 마음에
온종일 미소 짓는다

제사상의 향백(香栢)으로
여린 순과 뿌리
잊지 못할 관상용의 기쁨!

Day Lily Flower

In the wind and rain
Perennial grass that makes you forget your anxiety
In the sun it is the petal in which it bites
Be fresh and beautiful

A blade-thin, long leaves
I'm facing you in two rows
Dancing with each other

In the single stem flower bed
Funnel-shaped isochrome flowers are smilingly
With the ends splitting into several
In my mind, tired of waiting
I smile all day

In the scent white of the sacrificial table
A soft root
The joy of the unforgettable ornamental use!

연화(蓮花)

진흙탕 물속에서

꽃대 길게 솟아올라
수면 위로
부처님 미소 피워 올린
저 연꽃 송이들

넓은 잎으로
빗방울 정화하며

삶의 그리움을
수면에 그린다.

Lotus Flower

In the muddy water

A long rise of flower beds
Above the surface
The Buddha's smile
Those lotus clusters

Broadly
Purifying raindrops

The longing of life
Draw on the surface of water.

카라꽃 그대

제2부

한라산의 눈꽃

백설의 순결한 세계가
억겁의 세월을 달려와
맑고 하얀빛 부서지는
겨울 한라의 눈꽃 잔치

재스민꽃

한 송이 꽃을 잊지 못하네

밤하늘의 눈부신 별처럼
그 청순한 눈빛
다소곳한 몸짓
불같은 감수성을 그리며

길 떠나는 나그네처럼
그 향기를 사랑했네

순백의 꽃
화려함은 없어도
무더위 이겨내고
슬픔에 젖은 눈망울로
미련 없이 떠나버리는 꽃

여름마다 고운 모습으로
나타나 무뎌졌던 감성을
되찾아 주는 꽃.

Jasmine Flower

I can't forget a flower

Like a dazzling star in the night sky
That innocent look
A rather cluttered gesture
With a fiery sensitivity

Like a street-leaving stranger
I loved the scent

A pure white flower
Without the glamour
I'm gonna get through the heat
With a sad eye
A flower that leaves without hesitation

Every summer in a fine manner
And then you're gonna have to give me
Flowers to be recovered.

한라산의 눈꽃

한라산 기슭에
은빛 설화(雪花)가 만발하면

나뭇가지에 온통
눈꽃이 피어
순백의 향연(饗宴)

푸른 구상나무가 빚어낸
한겨울의 싱그러움이
한라의 숲을 뒤덮은 눈꽃과
조화롭게 피어나네!

칼바람 눈보라 속에서도
꿋꿋한 나무들의 자태는
겨울의 생동감을 더하고

정신없이 걸어야 하는 조급증에도
낯선 산길에 마음이 설렌다

산행 굽이굽이
거친 내 숨소리가
백록담에선 들리지 않고

아스라한 흔적을 간직한
밋밋한 산길에도
용암 흘러내리며
태어나던 백설의 순결한 세계가
억겁의 세월을 달려와
맑고 하얀빛 부서지는
겨울 한라의 눈꽃 잔치

지금도 살아 숨 쉬는 듯하네!

Snowflakes of Mt. Halla

At the foot of Mt. Halla
When the silver snowflakes is full

All over the branches
Snowflakes
The Feast of the Pure White

Green-specified
The freshness of winter
With the snowflakes that covered Halla's forest
It's blooming in harmony!

In the cold wind and snowstorm
The shape of the trees that are strong
Adding to the vibrant winter

I'm not sure I'm going to have to walk
I am thrilled by the strange mountain path

A mountain bend
My breath is rough
It's unheard In the white wall

With a trace of asra
In the plain mountains
Lava-flowing
The innocent world of snow white
I'm going to run through the years
Clear white-broken
Winter Halla's Snow Flower Festival

I think it's still breathing alive!

능소화

창밖 울타리에
걸쳐 있는 능소화
주황빛으로 물든 꽃송이
송이송이 매달려

한여름 무더위에
가지 엮으며 친구 만들고
늘어진 가지로 해를 잡으려
수줍어 미소 짓는 능소화 연정

세상 구경이 하고 싶어
주홍 등불 켜고

고고하고 화려함을
가슴에 안은 채
저녁노을을 바라보며
꽃길을 가련다.

Trumpet Creeper

Out the window on the fence
Spanning trumpet creeper
Orange-colored flower buds
The flower cluster hang on

In the midsummer heat
Wearing branches, making friends
To take the sun with a loose branch
A shy smile of nepotism

I want to see the world
With the scarlet lamp on

The high and the glamorous
With a hug in his chest
Looking at the sunset
The flower path is a path.

감꽃 목걸이

라일락 향기 저무는 오월
골목마다 감꽃이
떨어질 때면
어릴 적 옛 동무가 생각난다

애틋한 마음
늘 곁에 있었지만
감꽃 목걸이
예쁘게 만들어
그대에게 걸어주지 못했다

쳐다보면 숨이 막혀
어쩌지 못하는 순간처럼
그렇게 떠나보내고

추억이 강물처럼 흐를 때
감꽃 향기 유난히 흩날리는
오월이 오면
오래오래 그리워했다.

Persimmon Flower Necklace

May with a Laylac Scent
Persimmon flowers
When it falls
I remember an old companion as a child

A hearty heart
I've always been there
Persimmon necklace
Make it beautiful
I did not hang your neck

I'm choking when I look at it
Like a moment of inability
So you let him go

When memories flow like rivers
Persimmon-scented
May comes
I missed it for a long time.

청양고추꽃

하얀 별 같은 작은 꽃 매달아
벌 나비 모으더니
아기 손가락 같은 초록 열매가
주렁주렁

극심한 가뭄에 말라붙는 청양고추
작은 고추가 맵다는 속담 따라

보신탕에도 청양고추 듬뿍
된장찌개에도 청양고추 가득

한여름
뜨거운 칼국수에
청양고추 잔뜩 썰어 넣어
땀을 뻘뻘

후덥지근한 무더위에
아저씨 아주머니
청양고추 없이는
못살아!

Cheongyang Red Pepper Flower

Hang a little flower like a white star
I collected bees and butterflies
Green berries like baby fingers
The berries hang around

Cheongyang pepper dried in extreme drought
According to the saying that the little red pepper is spicy

Boshintang has plenty of Cheongyang red pepper
Doenjang stew also has Cheongyang red pepper

Midsummer
In hot kalguksu
Cut in a lot of Cheongyang red pepper
Sweaty

In the hot heat
Uncle and aunt
Without Cheongyang red pepper
You can't live!

프리지어꽃

그대 그리워
노랑 프리지어꽃을 보고
내 마음 환하게 봄이 되었다

어느덧
마음속에 흥건히
황홀감에 젖어

그대라는 빛 하나에
자꾸만 눈길이 가는 프리지어

프리지어꽃 빛처럼
노란빛 청순함으로

쓸쓸해하는 이 가슴
미소 지을 수 있으리!

Freesia Flower

I miss you
I saw yellow freesia flowers
It was spring in my heart

A short time
In my heart
In ecstasy

In the light of you
A freesia that keeps on getting the eye

Like a freesia flower
With a yellow purity

This lonely heart
You can smile!

베고니아꽃

파르르 떠는 연분홍 꽃잎
그 안에 품은 향기
가슴에 스며드는 그리움

끊임없이 꽃을 피워
기쁨을 물들이는 베고니아

다소곳이 가슴에 품은 슬기
도톰한 이파리마다 돋우어
피어오를지도 모를 이상을 향하여
일렁이는 이야기

빨강, 노랑, 분홍, 흰색으로
조화롭게 등불 되어

붉은 열정을 품고
속살 같은 꽃잎이 지면서도
빙긋이 웃으며 익어가던
하루의 고요!

Begonian Flower

A puffy pink petal
The scent in it
The longing that permeates the heart

Incessantly flowering
A joy-staining begonia

A bit of wisdom in his chest
Every thick leaf
To the ideal that might rise
A story of the wind

Red, yellow, pink, white
In harmony

With a red passion
The petal like the inside flesh is lost
Whether you're laughing and ripe
The silence of the day!

천일홍꽃

맑고 푸른 하늘 아래
노을빛이 물들 무렵에
피어난
선물 같은 한 송이 꽃

내 사랑 알알이 영글어
빨간 꽃, 분홍 꽃, 하얀 꽃
아롱다롱 맺힌 꽃
옹기종기 웃는 꽃

꽃잎 한 장 한 장
넘길 때마다
한 몸 되어 피어난 꽃
천년을 사는
불멸의 꽃

아쉬움과 사랑
그리움의 향기가 지켜주는
인연의 꽃.

Celestial Red Flower

Under the clear blue sky
At the time of the glow
Pierced
A gift of flowers

My love is beautiful
Red flowers, pink flowers, white flowers
A flower of flowers
A laughing flower

A petal sheet
Every time I turn it over
Flowers blooming in one body
Millennium-living
Immortal flower

Regret and love
With the scent of longing
Flowers of a relationship.

과꽃

자줏빛 꽃잎에
아침 이슬이 차다

불러보라
가을의 노래를
눈물 없이 서럽다

구름이 과꽃 위에
떠 있구나

저 구름의 노래는
고향의 노래일까

과꽃에 묻는다
고향의 소식은
언제 들리려나

산길 따라
추억 속에 두었을까
들려주렴!

Pericarp Flower

In purple petals
Have morning dew

Sing me
A song of autumn
Be sad without tears

Clouds over the pericarp flowers
You're floating

That cloud song
Is it a song from home?

Bury in pericarp flowers
The news of home is
When are you coming in?

Along the mountain path
Is it in memory?
Let me hear it!

여뀌꽃

푸른 줄 잎 위에
산들바람이
살랑살랑

숨소리도 나직이
가만히 다가서면
예쁜 모습에 반해버려

논둑 밭둑에서
개울가까지
펼쳐진 아름다움

어디서
이리 고운 임
품어볼 수 있을까!

Smartweed Flower

On the blue stripe
A breeze
Salang salang

A low breath
When you're close
You have a crush on a pretty face

On the bank of a paddy bank
To the creek
Unfolding beauty

Where?
A fine one
Can I have it?

며느리밑씻개풀꽃

아무리 시어머니가 미워도
머지않아 나도 시어머니가
된다는 것을 생각하면
미워할 수가 없습니다

아무리 며느리가 미워도
내 아들과 함께 살며
손주들을 낳는다고 생각하니
미워할 수가 없습니다

오늘부터 사랑합시다
시어머니든 며느리든
다 행복해지기 위해
사는 것 아니겠습니까?

A Wash-Brush under the Daughter-in-law

No matter how much she hates her mother-in-law
Soon, I'm not sure
The thought of being
I can't hate you

No matter how hateful your daughter-in-law
I live with my son
I think you have grandchildren
I can't hate you

Let's love her from today
Whether you're a mother-in-law or a daughter-in-law
To be happy
Is it not living?

카라꽃 그대

제3부

며느리밥풀꽃

설레는 마음으로
시집와
지아비를 사랑한 며느리
아들을 사랑한 시어머니

고마리꽃

시골 개울가
지천으로 널려있는 꽃
작아도 산뜻하고 청초하다

앙증스레 핀 꽃처럼
예쁜 꽃망울이 참 예뻐
눈 비비고 다시 본다

파란 보석과 붉은 보석이 섞여
벌 나비가 날아다니는 듯
고혹적인 아름다움을 내뿜는다

작은 꽃등이 수없이
개여울을 다 덮고도
쉼 없이 물길을 밝힌다.

Persicaria Thunbergii Flower

A country stream
Flowers strewn with earth
Be small and neat

Like a flower of a little
You look beautiful in a flower
I rub my eyes and look again

Blue jewels and red jewels
Like a bee butterfly flying around
Emit an alluring beauty

Numerous times a small flower lamp
The small stream is covered
The water is lit without rest.

며느리밥풀꽃

한여름에 꽃이 피고 지는
며느리밥풀꽃

설레는 마음으로
시집와
지아비를 사랑한 며느리
아들을 사랑한 시어머니

서로 맛있는 밥상을
차리려다가 생긴 질투
끝내 타협할 줄 몰라

다소곳이 꽃으로 환생하여
빨간 입술마다
밥알 두 개 물고

며느리밥풀꽃으로
시집살이하던
슬픈 전설을 일깨워

우리의 가슴 한구석에
애절한 그리움으로
늘 피어 있으리.

Daughter-in-law's Rice Plant Flower

Flowering in the middle of summer
Daughter-in-law's rice plant

With a thrilling heart
Marry
A daughter-in-law who loved a husband
Mother-in-law who loved her son

A delicious table
Jealousy from trying to set up
I can't compromise

She is reincarnated with flowers shamefully
Every red lip
Two grains of rice

As a daughter-in-law
Married
Reminds me of a sad legend

In the corner of our hearts
With a sad longing
She'll always bloom.

별꽃

날이 어두워지자
밤하늘의 별들이
저 멀리서 반짝반짝

소곤소곤 남몰래
사랑을 속삭이며
천상에서 내려와
풀밭에 살짝 주저앉는다

둘인 듯 하나의 꽃잎으로
서로 사랑하며
반짝이는 눈망울

어두운 땅에서
하얀 별꽃으로
청초하게 피어나리.

Star Flower

As the day darkens
The stars in the night sky
A far-off sparkle

A little snooping
Whispering love
Get down from heaven
Sink a little on the grass

As if it were two, with one petal
In love with each other
A glittering eye

In the dark land
White-starred
A neat bloom.

제비꽃

봄바람이 살랑살랑
봄날을 맞이하는데
능선 길 따라 제비꽃이
활짝 피어올라

별빛 총총한 밤에도
햇살 좋은 낮에도
양지바른 길가에서
올망졸망 미소 짓네

보랏빛 고운 자태에
내 마음을 빼앗겨
길섶에 쪼그리고 앉아
옛 이야기 듣노라니

대지의 꽃들은
피어있는 그대로
꽃향기를
사방으로 흩날리네!

Violet

Spring breezes
In the spring
Violets along the ridge
In full bloom

Even on a starlit night
In the sunny day
On the sunny side of the road
You're smiling all over

In a purple, fine figure
I'm taken away from me
Squatting on the street
Listening to the old story

The flowers on the earth
As it is
Flower scent
It's all over the place!

빨간 채송화

햇볕이 쨍쨍
갈증을 이겨내고자

도톰하게 자란 이파리
그 짙푸른 촉수

가까이 보면
열리는 이 마음

그 속에 감추어진 이야기
행복 슬픔

내 어린 시절
학교 가는 길가에
흔했던 꽃

절대 꺾이지 않는
앙증스러운 꽃

언제나
붉게 피어나
한여름을 견딘다.

Red Rose Moss

The sun is shining
To overcome thirst

A thick-grown leaves
The deep blue tentacles

At close range
This open mind

A story hidden in it
Happiness sorrow

My childhood
On the road to school
Common flower

Never-breaking
A dainty flower

Always
Red-floating
I endure the summer.

꽃무릇꽃

하늬바람 살랑살랑
생각나고 그립다

붉은 가시 왕관 모양의 꽃
화려한 자태

열매를 맺을 수 없어
겨우내 푸른 잎으로 지내다가
봄에 새싹이
나왔다가 사라지고

여름에 다시 꽃대가 올라와
가을에 애절하게
그리움의 꽃으로 피었네

아, 보고파라

꽃과 이파리가
만날 수 없는 짝사랑 설화(說話)
오늘도 잊지 않고 기억하리니.

Flowering Flower

The sloppy breeze is blowing
Remember and miss

A red thorn crown
A splendid figure

Can't bear fruit
I'm just gonna stay blue
Spring bud
And then they came out and disappeared

The flower beds come up again in the summer
In the fall sadly
I'm blooming with nostalgia

Oh, I miss you

Flower and leaves
Unrequited love tales that you can't meet
I will remember today.

금계국꽃

길가에서 만나는
노란빛 파노라마
무리 지어
길목마다 지천으로 피어

어둡던 생각도
답답한 심정도
바람에 한들한들

네 살랑거리는 자태에
발걸음도 가볍게
자동차도 천천히
잠자리도 느릿느릿.

Golden Wave Flower

Meet by the side of the road
Yellow panorama
In a group
Bloom in the stream of the road

A dark thought
A frustrating degree of feeling
The wind is sore

In your sloppy form
Lightly in step
Car slow
The dragonfly is slow.

유채꽃

설렘이 다가와
파도가 일렁이듯

봄바람에
나무가 춤을 추듯

노랗게 물든 꽃물결이
가깝게 밀려오네

무리 지어 핀 꽃이여
이른 봄 산들바람에
누구를 찾으려
저리도 몸부림칠까

노랗게 물든 사연
유채꽃이여
상큼한 요정이 되어
춤을 추어라.

Rape Flower

A thrill is coming
Like waves

In the spring breeze
Like a tree dancing

The yellow-colored flower
It's coming close

A group of flowers
In the early spring breeze
Find someone
Will you struggle with that?

A yellow story
Canola flower
In a fresh fairy
Dance.

군자란꽃

아침저녁으로 물 주어
애지중지 귀하게 키운
우리 집 군자란꽃
한 아름 꺾어

이런저런 아픔으로
상처 입은 인연(因緣)에
내미는 따스한 손

그 손에 담긴
고귀한 군자란꽃

우아하게 피었네!

Arbor Flower

Water for breakfast and evening
Adored and precious
My house of arbor
Bend a little

With pain and pain
In the wounded relationship
A warm hand

In its hand
Noble arbor

It's gracefully blooming.

골무꽃

옛날 어려웠던 시절에
어머니가
다 헤진 옷을 기워 입히려고
시집올 때 가져온 반짇고리

밤새 호롱불 주위에서
골무를 끼고 그렇게
가족을 위해
아픔을 무릅쓰고
기도를 하셨다

그럴 때마다
골무가 있어
빈자리를 채운다

산행 길에 오르다가
보랏빛 골무꽃을 보고
그 옛날을 못 잊어
어머니 생각이 났다

비바람
한여름 무더위 속에서도
자신을 위해서는
한 마디도 하지 않는 골무꽃.

Thimble Flower

In the old days of hardship
My mother
I'm trying to get you dressed
Workbasket brought in from marriage

All night around the holong fire
With thimbles and so on
For the family
At the risk of pain
Prayed

Every time
Have thimbles
Fill the vacancy

On the mountain trail
I saw a purple thimble flower
I can't forget the old days
I thought of my mother

Rain and wind
In the middle of the summer
For oneself
A thimble flower that doesn't say a word.

대나무꽃

60여 년마다
보리 이삭처럼
피는 꽃

보는 사람에게
행운을 가져오는
신비의 꽃

일생에
한번 보기 힘든
전설의 꽃

꽃이 필 때는
줄기와 뿌리가
사라지는 꽃

치열한 생존 끝에
피고 지는
아름다운 꽃.

Bamboo Flower

Every 60 years
Like barley ears
A blooming flower

To the viewer
Luck-inducing
A flower of mystery

In one's lifetime
Hard to see
A flower of legend

When flowers bloom
Stem and root
A fading flower

After a fierce survival
Defendant-declared
Beautiful flowers.

카라꽃 그대

제4부

드라쿨라시미아꽃

다양한 종류에
표정도 천차만별
살아 움직이는 듯
괴기스럽다.

금어초꽃(金魚草花)

꽃이 피면서
화려한 꽃으로도
모자라

꽃이 지면서
금붕어 모양을
보인다

욕망인가
탐욕인가!

Snapdragon Flower

With flowers blooming
With a splendid flower
In short

As the flowers fade
The goldfish shape
I see

Desire
Greed!

드라큘라시미아꽃

남미의 고산지대에서
주로 서식하는 원숭이 난초

3개의 긴 드라큘라 이빨
으스스하다

일 년 내내 피고 지는
꽃잎 속에
원숭이 얼굴이 숨어 있어

눈동자가 선명하고
웃는 모습을 보인다

오렌지 향기가
춤추는 소녀처럼 흩날리고

다양한 종류에
표정도 천차만별
살아 움직이는 듯
괴기스럽다.

Draculasimia Flower

In the alpine region of South America
A predominantly inhabited monkey orchid

Three long Dracula teeth
Be eerie

Blooming and loses all year
In petal
The monkey face is hiding

With clear eyes
Show a smile

Orange-scented
It's like a dancing girl, and it's scatter

In various species
A lot of facial expressions
As if it were moving
It's weird.

사과꽃

파란 하늘
해맑은 들녘의 아침
살짝이 찾아드는 봄

하얗게
나뭇가지에 피어나는 수줍은 미소
아련한 사과꽃의 향연

아, 봄의 유혹인가!
산색은 푸르고
일렁이는 초록 물결 사이로
사과꽃의 연분홍빛 밀어

대롱대롱
앙증스럽게 매달려

사과나무마다 넘실거리는
붉은 사과의 연가.

Apple Flower

Blue sky
A sunny morning
Spring to find a little

Whitely
A shy smile on a branch
A feast of faint apple flowers

Oh, the temptation of spring!
The color is blue
Between the rolling green waves
The pale pink of the apple flower

Daelong daelong
Hang on a little bit

A fluttering of apple trees
The red apple's song.

개불알꽃

어느 봄날
양지바른 산기슭에
작은 꽃나무로 태어나
개불알을 품는다

앙증스러운 꽃
작아서 예쁜 풀꽃

주머니 모양
요강 모양
새빨간 공 모양

이름만 떠들썩한 소문에
겸연쩍은 웃음이 가득

쪼그리고 앉아
자세히 보니
상큼한 꽃향기는 나지 않고

오래 보니
숲속의 요정인 양
쉽게 시들지 않네!

Moccasin Flower

One spring day
At the foot of a sunny mountain
Born of a small flower tree
Hold a lady's slipper

A dainty flower
A small, pretty grass

Pocket shape
Lumbar shape
Red ball shape

I'm not sure if you're gonna get a name
A full of humbling laughter

Squat down
I can see closely
The fresh flower smell does not come out

I've seen it for a long time
A fairy in the woods
It's not easily withering!

은방울꽃

신비스럽다
바람이 불면
흔들리는 요령(鐃鈴)이 된다

백옥의 순수함
차마 만지지 못하고

올망졸망
여미어 도사린 긴 그리움 풀고

송알송알
몸을 뒤척이는
딸랑 소리 들리는 듯

은방울꽃
서로 마주 보고

스스럼없이
말을 주고받을 수 있어
행복해하네!

Silver-Drop Flower

Be mysterious
When the wind blows
It becomes a faltering trick

The purity of white flower
Without touching it

Olmanzol net
I'm gonna go through the long longing

Song al-song
Torsioning
Like a clatter

Silver-drop flower
Face to face

Without hesitation
I can talk to and receive
I'm happy!

층층이꽃

연분홍빛 꽃송이가
층마다
군집으로 피어

층층이 올라가듯
내려가고
내려가듯 올라가네

위아래 질서 있고
사이좋게 꽃 피워

탐스럽게
열매 열리네!

Stratified Flower

A pink flower bud
Per floor
A pile of flowers

As the floor rises
Down
It goes down

Up and down in order
Make a good flower

Covetously
The fruit is opening!

기생꽃(妓生花)

별 모양의 꽃으로
작은 키에
앙증맞은 모습이

하얀 꽃보다
더 진한 향취를 주고

순백의 아름다운 모습은
꽃 같은 마음을 주네

꽃 모양의 화관을 머리에 얹어
처음 만났을 때
그 모습이 예뻐

꽃을 보는 순간
고운 모습은 그리움을 주고
고운 사람에겐 기다림을 주네!

Arctic Starflower

In a star-shaped flower
At a small height
A dainty figure

Be a white flower
Give a richer scent

The beautiful appearance of pure white
They give you a flowery heart

The flower-shaped corolla is on put on the head
When I first met him
You look pretty

The moment you see the flowers
The fineness gives me longing
You're waiting for a fine man!

해오라비난초꽃

아름답고 독특한
해오라비난초꽃

그대를 바라보네
꿈에서라도 만나고 싶네

하얀빛으로
날아갈 듯
학의 모양을 한
해오라비난초꽃으로 피어나

어디론가
누구에겐가
날아갈 듯 서 있네

그립고 사랑스러운 그대에게
새가 되어
다가가리라.

Habenaria Radiata Flower

Beautiful and unique
Habenaria radiata flower

I look at you
I want to meet you in my dreams

Whitely
Flyingly
In the shape of a crane
It blooms with the habenaria radiata flower

Somewhere
To whom?
You're standing there like a fly

I miss you and I love you
A bird
I'll approach you.

게발선인장꽃

내 삶의 촉을 틔워
게의 발을 흉내 내며
사막의 길을 가고 있다

불타는 사랑은
붉은 꽃으로 분출하여
멈출 줄을 몰라

내일을 소망하며

이슬 한 방울에
갈증을 해소하고

공기 정화용으로
생존을 영위하네!

Crab Cactus Flower

I'm not gonna let you know
Imitating the crab's foot
Be on the path of the desert

Burning love
Erupt into red flowers
I don't know how to stop

In hopes of tomorrow

A drop of dew
Depleting thirst

For air purification
You're surviving!

감자꽃

감자꽃이 필 때는
은근히 예쁘다

신기해서
자세히 본다

혼자가 아닌
군집으로 피어
흰 꽃, 연보라 꽃
감자가 주렁주렁

가슴 가득히
차오르는 여유로움으로

꽃말처럼
그대를 따라가리!

Potato Flower

When potatoes bloom
Be a little pretty

In a curious way
Take a closer look

Not alone
Flowers bloom in bundles
White flower, lotus flower
A potatoes are buried in clusters

Full of chest
With a full ease

Like a flower language
I'll follow you!

카라꽃 그대

제5부

성에꽃

태양이 떠오르면
성인(聖人) 같은 몸짓
슬픔을 갈무리하며
흘린 눈물방울

소나무꽃

해마다
봄이 오면
꽃을 피우고 싶다

소나무의 봄은
세기(世紀)마다
오는 봄

오랜 세월
솔가지에 걸린
솔잎 향기에 취해

오래지 않아
기품 있게 머물던
그대의 세월에도

홍조 띤 고귀한 꽃을
보는 날이
드물지 않으리!

Pine Flower

Year by year
When spring comes
I want to bloom

The spring of pines
Every century
Coming spring

Long years
Pine-branched
In the pine needles aroma

Not long
A graceful stay
In your years

A red-tinged noble flower
The day you see
Not uncommon!

짚신나물꽃

짚신 매달고
길 떠나던 날

발길 닿는 곳이라면
그곳이 어디든지

열매에 달린 갈고리가
짚신에 달라붙어
다니는 곳마다
씨를 뿌리는구나!

새싹의 모양이
용의 이빨을 닮고

이파리가 해독제로 쓰여
목숨을 구하네!

이제라도 짚신 신고
발길 가는 대로

노래 부르며
걸어볼까!

Agrimonia Pilosa Flower

With a straw
The day you left

Wherever you get to
Wherever it is

A hook on a fruit
Cling to a straw
Wherever you go
You sow seeds!

The shape of the bud
Like a dragon's teeth

The leaves are used as antidotes
Save your life!

I'm wearing a straw now
On the way

Singing
Let's walk!

고구마꽃

여러해살이풀
고구마꽃을 보셨나요?

100년에 한 번
여름에 핀다는
고구마꽃의 꽃말은
'행운'

좀처럼 보기 힘든 꽃이기에
행운을 가져오는 희귀한 꽃이자
좋은 일이 생길 길조 꽃

언젠가
고구마꽃 보시고
자신에게도 행운을!

Sweet Potato Flower

Perennial grass
Did you see the sweet potato flower?

Once every 100 years
I'm gonna be in the summer
The flower words of sweet potato flowers
'Luck'

It's a rare flower
It's a rare flower that brings good fortune
A good flower to come

Someday
See the sweet potato flowers
Good luck to yourself!

바람꽃

살랑살랑
나뭇잎 흔드는
바람 소리

살아있는
풀잎의 숨소리

낙엽 이불을 뚫고
삐죽이 고개 내민
끈질긴 그 목숨

그대만이 볼 수 있는
외로운 바람꽃
다하지 못한 사랑.

Wind Flower

Salang salang
Leaf-shaking
Wind sound

Living
The breathing of grass leaves

Through the fallen bed
A pouting head
The persistent life

Only you can see
A lonely wind flower
Love that I have not done.

앵무새꽃

수많은 꽃 중에서
가장 예쁜 꽃 중의 하나인
앵무새꽃은

하늘로
비상하는
앵무새를 닮았을까!

앵무새가 환생하여
전설의 꽃이 된 걸까!

앵무새가
꽃을 따라
열렬한 사랑을 하고 싶어
앵무새꽃으로 피었나!

Parrot Flower

Among many flowers
One of the most beautiful flowers
Parrot flower

Into the sky
In flight
Like a parrot!

A parrot is reincarnated
Is it a flower of legend?

Parrot
Along the flowers
I want to make a passionate love
Is it a parrot flower?

석류꽃

지울 수 없는
석류꽃의 원숙미(圓熟美)
가슴에 찍혀

그곳에서 헤어나지 못하던
까마득한 사춘기 시절

정겨움 가득했던
지난 세월의 뒤안길에서
달아오른 붉은 여성의 꽃
그 열매

황홀하여라
해마다 7월이면
그리운 듯
향기로운 꽃향기에 빠져
세월을 잊는다.

Pomegranate Flower

Undeletable
The Precocious Beauty of Pomegranate Flowers
On the chest

I'm not gonna get out of there
A period of puberty

Full of heart
In the back streets of the past years
A flower of a red woman
The fruit

Be ecstatic
Every July
As if I missed you
In the scent of fragrant flowers
Forget the years.

참깨꽃 밭에서

깊어가는 여름날
바람 불어 좋은 날에
호미자락으로
참깨밭을 일군다

한여름의 빛살이
땀방울로 흐르면

삶의 공간에
향기로운 참깨꽃 향기 흩날려
기대감을 품게 하네

감출 수 없는 그 사랑
살짝 고개 숙인
연보랏빛 꽃송이들

올망졸망 함께 피어
그리움으로 쏟아지리!

In the Sesame Flower Field

A deep summer day
On a good day
With a homi
Work sesame fields

Midsummer light
You're gonna sweat

In the space of life
It scatters scentful sesame flowers.
It's a big deal

The unscathed love
A little bow
Violet flower buds

A full-blown blossoms
I'll be pouring out of nostalgia!

빨간입술꽃

가장
키스하고 싶은 꽃
빨간입술꽃

요염한 입술로
누군가를
유혹하기 위해

립스틱을 바르고
도톰하게 내미는 입술로

살짝 입맞춤하는
그 뜨거운 꽃 입술!

Red Lip Flower

A fabulous
A flower I want to kiss
Red lip flower

With a amorous lips
I'm gonna have to tell someone
To seduce

With lipstick
With thick lips

Slightly kissing
The hot flower lips!

금은화

준초(峻峭)한 산야에
꽃봉오리로 수(繡)를 놓는다

겨울을 견딘 인동초
5월이 오면
흰빛으로 피어
노란빛으로 변하는 금은화

산새 울음소리
은은한 꽃 향이 깃드는 곳에

인동(忍冬)이 우려진
잎 차 한잔으로
햇살같이 싱그러운
사랑의 이야기 꽃피우네!

해마다
금은화(金銀花) 필 때면
임을 찾아

잊을 수 없는
지난 시절 향기에
그리움을 찾는다.

Lonicera Flower

In the high mountainous area
Place the embroidery with the bud

The honeysuckle that endured winter
May comes
White-colored
A yellow-colored lonicera flower

A mountain bird cry
Where the subtle flower scents

Honeysuckle-expressed
With a cup of leaf tea
Sunny and fresh
The story of love blossoms!

Year by year
When lonicera flowers bloom
Find him

Unforgettable
In the past scent
I look for nostalgia.

부추꽃

언제나
함께 있는 우리는

바람이 불 때마다
순수함으로 다가오는
고결한 저 꽃무리

인파가 모일 때마다
사랑의 향기 가득

일렁이는 꽃물결 속에
아름다운 추억을
점점이 쏟아 놓은
그리움의 물결.

Leek Flower

Always
We're together

Every time the wind blows
Coming with purity
A noble flowering herd

Every time a crowd gathers
A full scent of love

In the wavy wave of flowers
To make a beautiful memory
Dotted
A wave of longing.

성에꽃

엄동설한의 기온에서
어려웠던 시절

겨울을 알리러
유리창 안쪽에 선연히 맺힌
미세한 빙화(氷花)

태양이 떠오르면
성인(聖人) 같은 몸짓
슬픔을 갈무리하며
흘린 눈물방울

혹한의 어둠이 오면
우리가 사는 세상 만상
따뜻한 마음으로
다시 그려내는
끝없는 수림(樹林).

Frost Flower

At the temperature of the hard snowy winter
A difficult time

To announce the winter
Drawing it on the inside of the window
Microscopic icebergs

When the sun rises
Saintlike gestures
With sorrow
A shed teardrop

When the darkness of cold comes
The world we live in
With a warm heart
Repainting
Endless forest.

카라꽃 그대

초판인쇄 2021년 2월 20일   초판발행   2021년 2월 25일

지은이   장현경
펴낸이   장현경   펴낸곳   엘리트출판사
등록일   2013년 2월 22일 제2013-10호

지은이   장현경
펴낸이   장현경   펴낸곳   엘리트출판사
등록일   2013년 2월 22일 제2013-10호

정가 11,000원

ISBN 979-11-87573-27-2 03810